Library of Congress Cataloging-in-Publication Data
Names: Antony, Steve, author, illustrator.
Title: Thank you, Mr. Panda / Steve Antony.
Description: First edition. | New York, NY : Scholastic Press, 2017.
Summary: Mr. Panda has presents for all his animal friends, but many of the gifts are not
quite right—but as little Lemur knows, it is the thought that counts. | Description based on print version
record and CIP data provided by publisher; resource not viewed.Identifiers: LCCN 2016051150 (print)
LCCN 2016050219 (ebook) | ISBN 9781338184952 | ISBN 9781338158366 (hardcover)
Subjects: LCSH: Pandas—Juvenile fiction. | Animals—Juvenile fiction. | Gifts—Juvenile fiction.
Gratitude—Juvenile fiction. | CYAC: Pandas—Fiction. | Animals—Fiction. | Gifts—Fiction.
Gratitude—Fiction.Classification: LCC PZ7.A632 (print) | LCC PZ7.A632 Th 2017 (ebook)
DDC [E]—dc23 | LC record available at https://lccn.loc.gov/2016051150

10 9 8 7 6 5 4 3 2 1          17 18 19 20 21

Printed in China  38
This edition first printing, October 2017

# Thank You, Mr. Panda

Steve Antony

Who are all
the presents
for, Mr. Panda?

My friends.

This is for Mouse.

A present for me, Mr. Panda?

It's the thought that counts.

But it's too big.

This is for Octopus.

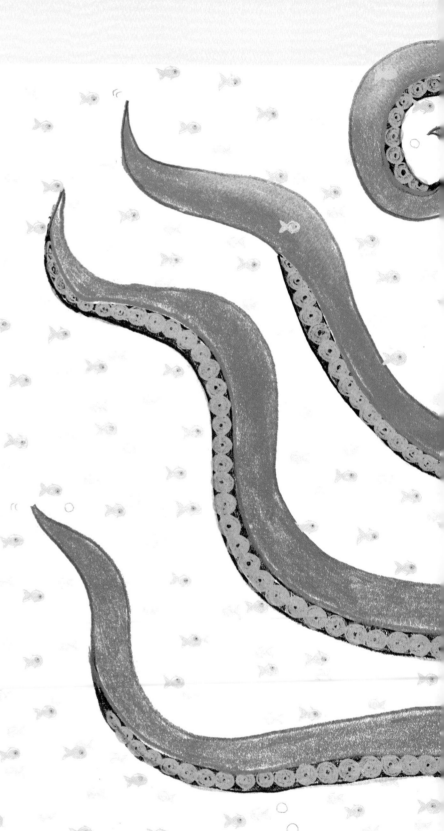

A gift for me,
Mr. Panda?

But I have eight legs.

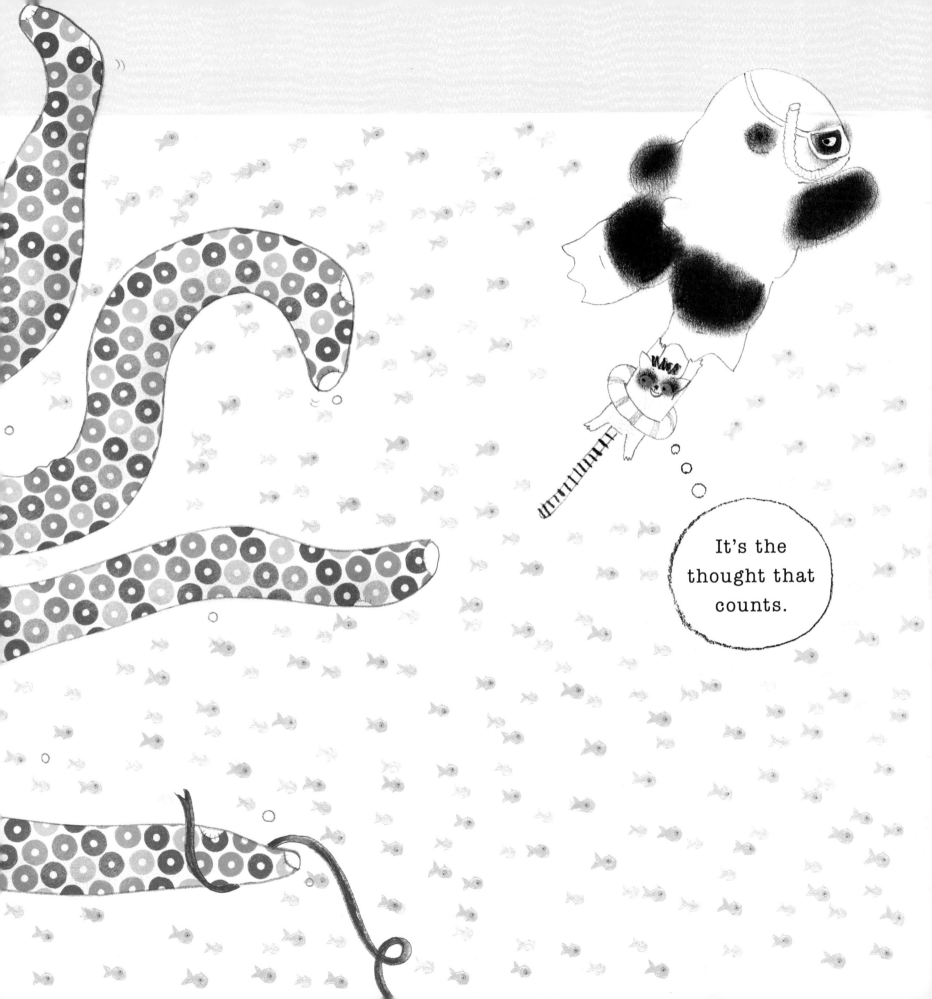

This is for Elephant.

I will open it later.

And this is for
Mountain Goat.

Something for me, Mr. Panda?

But it's too long.

It's the thought that counts.

Who is the
last present
for, Mr. Panda?

It's for you.

# Thank you, Mr. Panda!

You're welcome,
but remember . . .

...it's the thought that counts.